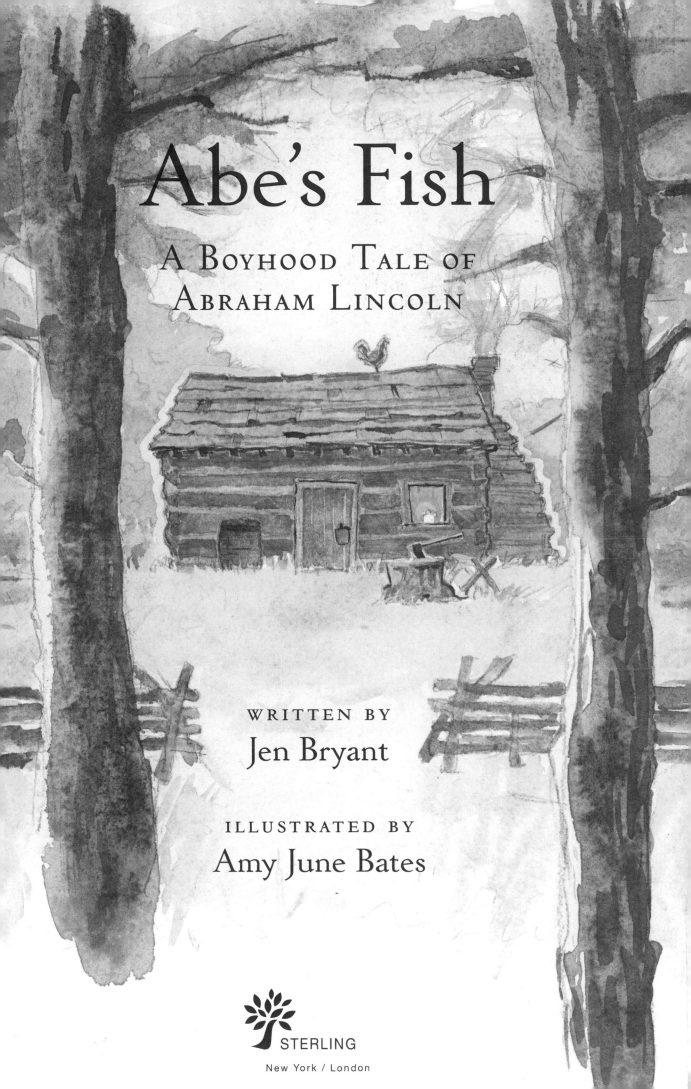

Abe's Fish

A Boyhood Tale of
Abraham Lincoln

WRITTEN BY
Jen Bryant

ILLUSTRATED BY
Amy June Bates

STERLING

New York / London

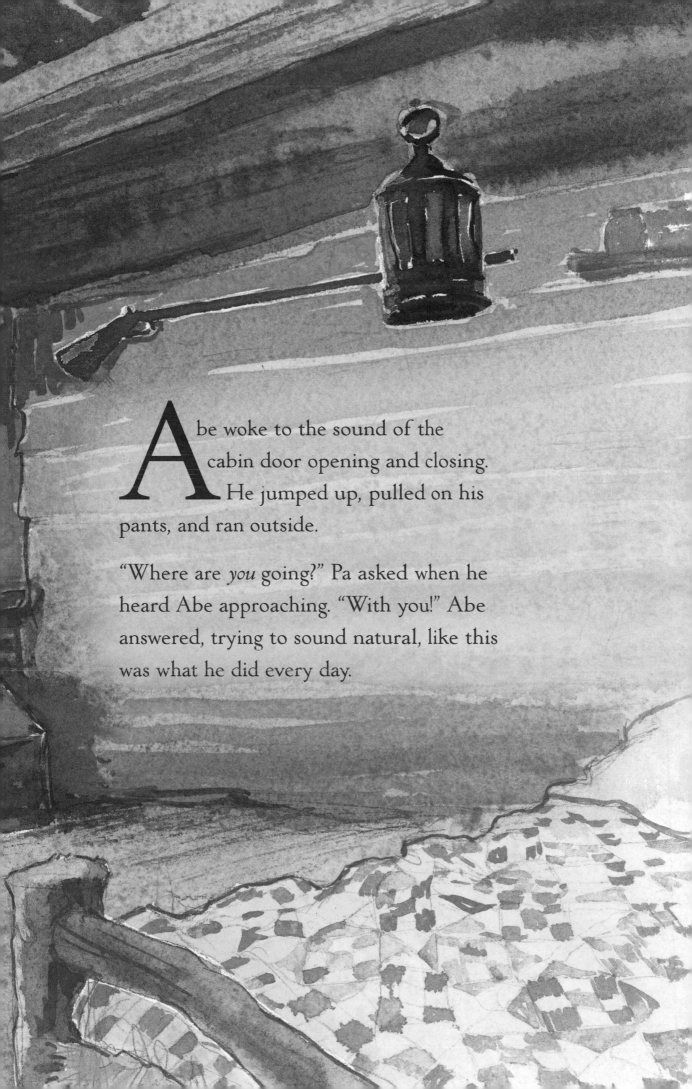

Abe woke to the sound of the cabin door opening and closing. He jumped up, pulled on his pants, and ran outside.

"Where are *you* going?" Pa asked when he heard Abe approaching. "With you!" Abe answered, trying to sound natural, like this was what he did every day.

Pa stopped. He put his axe on the ground.
Abe stood beside it, breathing hard.
"Go ahead then," Pa offered. "Go ahead
and lift it."

With both hands, Abe grasped the handle.
He pulled up-up-up until his wrists burned.
The axe was too heavy.

With one hand, Pa lifted the axe. With his
other hand, he gently squeezed Abe's
shoulder. "Maybe next time," said Pa, and
disappeared into the trees.

Abe picked up a rock and tossed it hard.
There was no need to hurry back to the
cabin. Abe was sure he'd be spending another
boring afternoon picking berries with his
sister, Sarah.

But Ma surprised him. "Why don't you
take your fishing pole over to Knob Creek—
see if you can catch us a fish for dinner?"
Abe did not have to be asked twice.
Compared to picking berries, fishing was
grown-up work. Besides, after several days
of turnip soup and little green apples, a fish
dinner sounded mighty fine!

It was a half-mile down the road to the best spot. Abe baited his hook, dropped his line, and settled himself on the bank.

Fish-fish-fish—Abe turned the word over and over again in his mind. *"Fish-fish-fish,"* he whispered to the water.

Abe loved words. He loved speaking them out loud. He loved writing them with a stick in the dirt. And on the days he went to school with Sarah, Abe loved reading them, too.

Tug-tug. Tug-*tug-tug!*

Abe tightened his grip.
He remembered what Pa had said:

"Hold steady and pull at just the right time."

Abe held steady. When his hands felt the
full weight of the fish, he yanked the pole
upward, swinging the line behind him.

"Gotcha!" he cried.

Abe had one worm left. He rolled it in a damp leaf and, smiling to himself, put it in his pocket.

A nice surprise for Sarah's pillow tonight.

The late-day sun warmed Abe's back and deepened the red of a ripe apple that hung by the roadside, just out of reach. Abe tried three times to poke it down with a stick, but the apple refused to drop.

I wish I was tall! he thought.

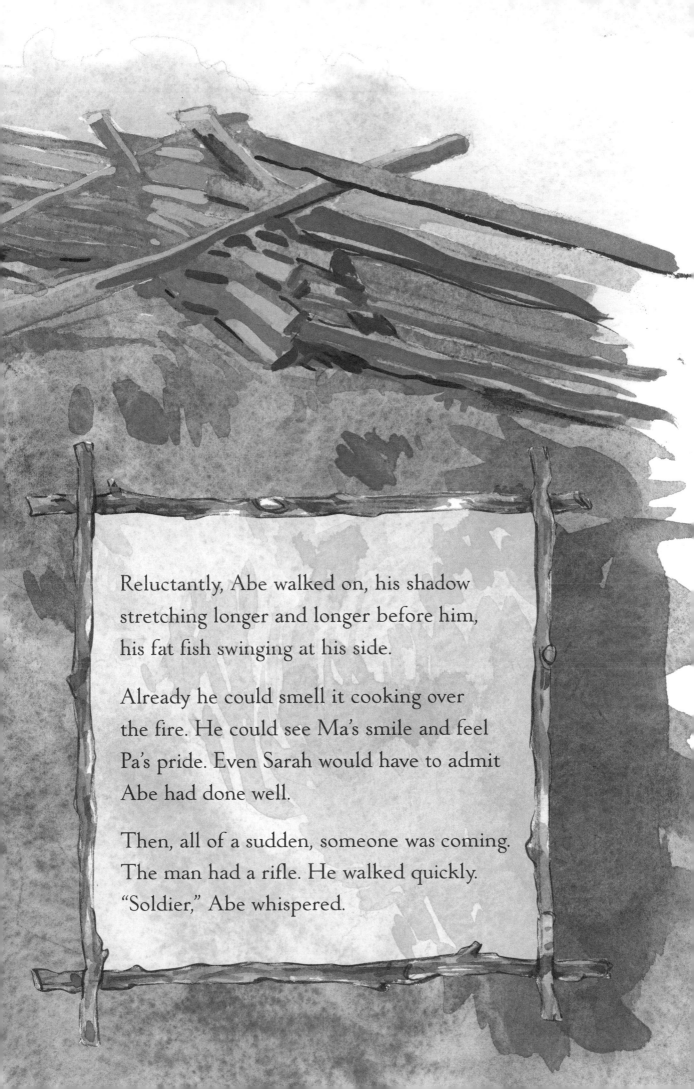

Reluctantly, Abe walked on, his shadow
stretching longer and longer before him,
his fat fish swinging at his side.

Already he could smell it cooking over
the fire. He could see Ma's smile and feel
Pa's pride. Even Sarah would have to admit
Abe had done well.

Then, all of a sudden, someone was coming.
The man had a rifle. He walked quickly.
"Soldier," Abe whispered.

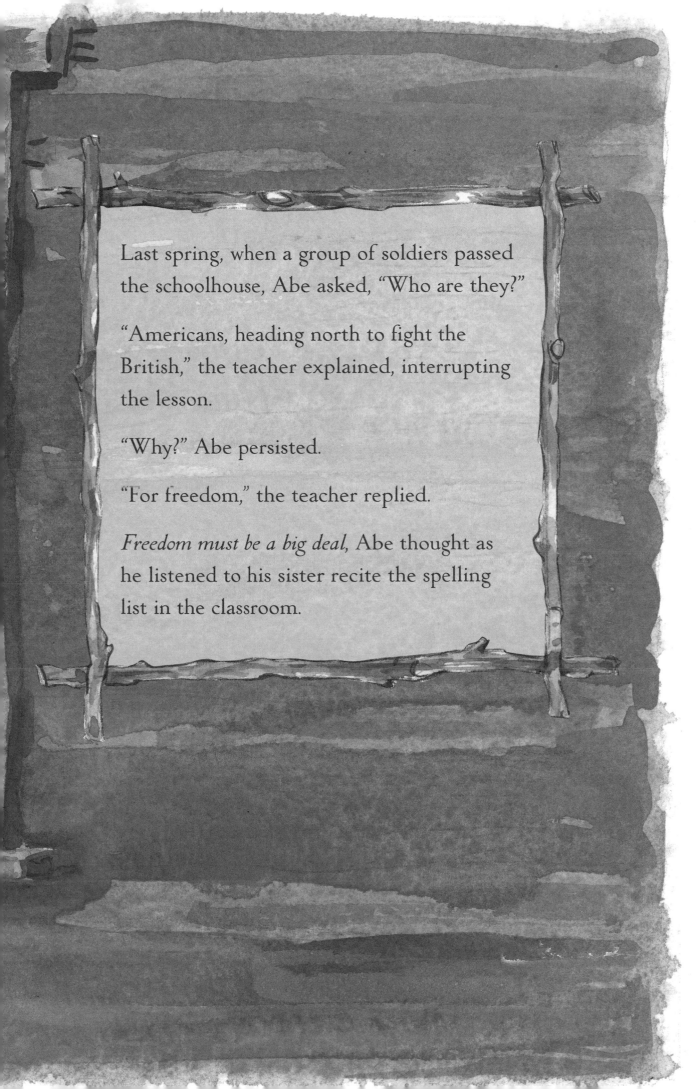

Last spring, when a group of soldiers passed the schoolhouse, Abe asked, "Who are they?"

"Americans, heading north to fight the British," the teacher explained, interrupting the lesson.

"Why?" Abe persisted.

"For freedom," the teacher replied.

Freedom must be a big deal, Abe thought as he listened to his sister recite the spelling list in the classroom.

Abe wondered about freedom. Once when
he'd put a cricket in a cage, it stopped
moving and chirping. But when Abe let it go,
it jumped quickly through the grass and
started singing again.

But people don't live in cages, thought Abe, *so
how could they not be free? Why would they need
to fight for freedom?*

Abe remembered now what Ma had said when he'd told her about the men:

"We must be good to the soldiers."

Now here was a real soldier, coming toward him. A stranger. Cautious, Abe moved aside.

"Hey there, boy," the soldier said, spreading his palms in front of him. "Don't be a-feared. I mean no harm to you or your fine fish."

Up close, Abe noticed the man's torn clothes, his worn-out boots, and thought, *He's poor like me.*

Abe saw, too, how the soldier looked at the fish. It was a hungry look.

"We must be good to the soldiers," Ma had said. Abe remembered the Bible stories she had read to him at night—and one in particular about a good Samaritan who helped a poor man on the road when others passed by.

Abe stared at his catch. He thought about how happy his family would be when they sat down to supper—a real fish supper— their first full meal in a week.

Abe sniffed. He shuffled his feet. He looked again at the fish. A long minute passed.

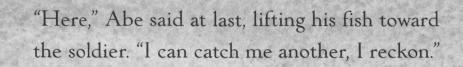

"Here," Abe said at last, lifting his fish toward the soldier. "I can catch me another, I reckon."

A weary smile spread across the man's face. "Thank you kindly!" he said, and started down the road again.

"Hey—wait!" Abe called after him. "Did you find freedom?"

The soldier turned. He fixed his gaze on something far away. "I reckon I did see it sometimes," he finally replied. "But other times, it seemed a long way off."

He waved to Abe and walked on.

The sun was low now—too low for Abe to go back to the creek and try to catch another fish. Ma would worry if he wasn't home by dark.

At the cabin, Sarah's disappointment greeted him. "Didn't *think* you'd catch anything," she said.

Abe looked down, shaking his head. "I caught a perch. But I gave it to a soldier on the road. He looked hungry."

"Well, so are we . . . did you think about *that?*" Sarah scolded.

"'Course I did!" Abe snapped back. "I just reckoned he needed it more than us, that's all."

Ma heard. She pulled another turnip off the shelf and sliced it into the steaming pot. "Go wash up, you two," she said, her voice firm, but not angry. Abe was pretty sure Ma would have given *her* fish to a hungry soldier.

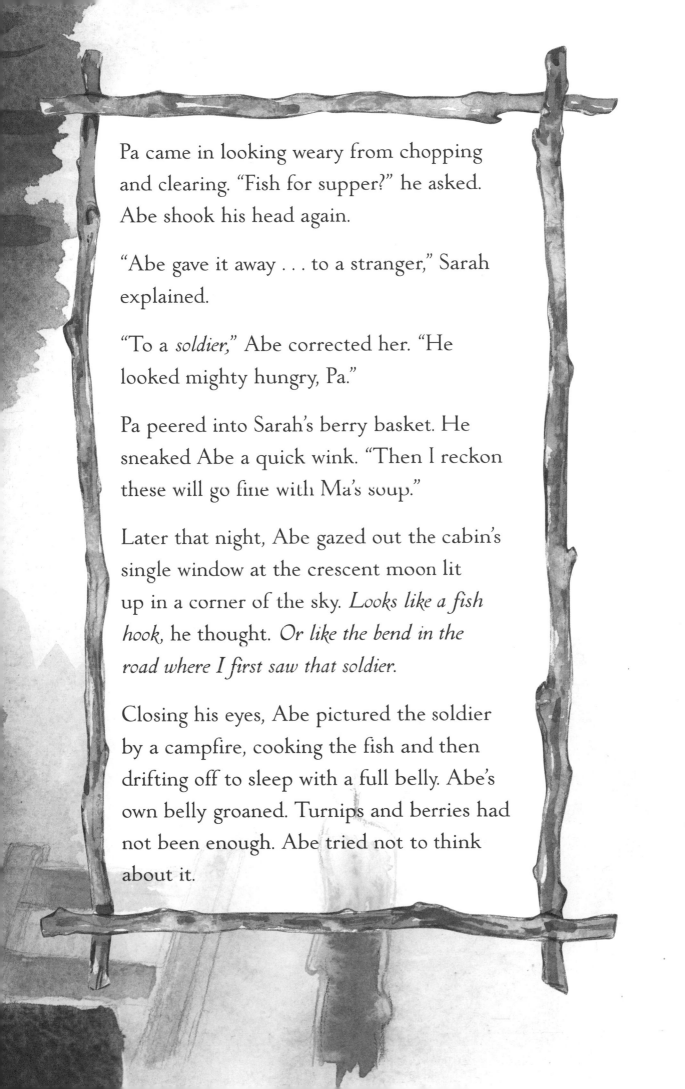

Pa came in looking weary from chopping and clearing. "Fish for supper?" he asked. Abe shook his head again.

"Abe gave it away . . . to a stranger," Sarah explained.

"To a *soldier*," Abe corrected her. "He looked mighty hungry, Pa."

Pa peered into Sarah's berry basket. He sneaked Abe a quick wink. "Then I reckon these will go fine with Ma's soup."

Later that night, Abe gazed out the cabin's single window at the crescent moon lit up in a corner of the sky. *Looks like a fish hook*, he thought. *Or like the bend in the road where I first saw that soldier.*

Closing his eyes, Abe pictured the soldier by a campfire, cooking the fish and then drifting off to sleep with a full belly. Abe's own belly groaned. Turnips and berries had not been enough. Abe tried not to think about it.

Instead, he whispered the words he'd learned
to spell in school:

> "*D-o-g . . . DOG.*
> *D-i-g . . . DIG.*
> *D-i-s-h . . . DISH.*
> *F-i-s-h . . . FISH.*"

Dang! That made his stomach growl again.

With his finger, he wrote words onto the
slate of night:

> *F-o-g . . . FOG.*
> *F-l-a-g . . . FLAG.*

Pa said the flag stood for freedom. But what
did freedom *look* like? Abe still couldn't quite
picture it. Even the soldier hadn't seemed
too sure.

FREEDOM. He tried the word out in his
mouth. It was a big word, Abe could tell.
The next time he went to school, he would
practice writing it.

Someday, Abe thought, *it might be a good word to know.*

Author's Note

Although much has been written about the adult Abraham Lincoln, the sixteenth president of the United States who kept the country united and abolished slavery, we know very little about his earliest years. Most of what we do know has been passed down to us through oral history and through Abe's own telling. The story *Abe's Fish* grew out of the following passage from his first official biography. Published in 1890, it was written by John G. Nicolay and John Hay, who were Abe's private secretaries during his presidency:

Once, when asked what he remembered about the war with Great Britain, he replied:

"'Nothing but this. I had been fishing one day and caught a little fish which I was taking home. I met a soldier in the road, and, having been always told at home that we must be good to the soldiers, I gave him my fish.'"

—ABRAHAM LINCOLN: A HISTORY

It was a great challenge for me to spin these few lines into a book that you'd enjoy, one that I hope has made you want to learn more. As you read *Abe's Fish*, you probably had questions about Abe, his family, his home, and our country at this time. I had many questions, too, as I began this book.

What was Abe's mother like?

At the time of her marriage to Thomas Lincoln, Abe's mother, Nancy Hanks, was described by neighbors as "a handsome young woman of twenty-three, of appearance and intellect superior to her lowly fortunes." Unlike many working-class women of her time, Nancy could read quite well, but sources conflict about her ability to write. (She made an "X" in place of her signature on at least one official document.) Even so, it appears that she did teach Abe and Sarah some of their letters and instructed her husband, Thomas, on how to write his name.

The life of a frontier family was hard, and Nancy's days were filled with cooking, cleaning, and mending. At night, however, the family gathered by the fire and listened as she read from the only book the family owned, the Holy Bible. We can't know for certain if she read to them about the Good Samaritan, but it's likely that she did.

Later, when the Lincolns moved to Indiana, Nancy died suddenly of milk fever, a disease caused by drinking milk from cows that had eaten a poisonous root. Grief-stricken, nine-year-old Abe made the pegs for the coffin in which his "angel mother" was buried.

What happened then?

About a year later, Thomas Lincoln married a Kentucky widow, Sarah (Sally) Bush Johnston. Fortunately for Abe, his new mother also loved books and brought along a small collection from her former home. Although Sally herself was uneducated, she recognized Abe's intelligence and encouraged him to read and write as often as he could. Just before he became president, Abe made a special trip back home to thank Sally for all she had done for him.

What sort of man was Thomas Lincoln?

Abe's father was generally "an easy going man" who nonetheless became "a formidable adversary" when angered. Thomas Lincoln had grown up used to hard times: when just six years old, Thomas had witnessed his own father's murder and was barely saved by his older brother from being kidnapped. As a young man, Thomas wandered from farm to farm doing odd jobs until he was hired as an apprentice in the carpenter's shop owned by Nancy's uncle, Joseph Hanks.

Abe's father was of average height, with dark hair and skin and a strong, muscular build. Abe inherited most of these traits, but he grew much taller than his father . . . much taller, in fact, than most men of that time: "I am," Abe wrote to a friend in 1860, "six feet four inches, nearly; lean in flesh, weighing on average one hundred and eighty pounds; dark complexion, with coarse black hair and grey eyes." In the wilds of Indiana, both Thomas and Abe were known for their skill with an axe, their stamina behind the plow, and their strength as wrestlers.

Other than his older sister Sarah, did Abe have other siblings?

When Abe was three years old, Nancy Lincoln gave birth to a baby boy, who lived only a few days. Later, after the family had moved to Indiana and Thomas Lincoln had remarried, Abe's stepmother, Sally, brought along three children of her own. Abe's two stepsisters, Elizabeth and Matilda, and his stepbrother, John, seemed to have gotten along very well. Abe also spent a lot of time with his older cousin, Dennis Hanks, who eventually married Abe's stepsister Elizabeth.

Where is Knob Creek? How long did Abe and his family live there?

Thomas Lincoln cultivated about 30 acres of the almost 230 acres at Knob Creek Farm. Located just a few miles from Hodgenville, Kentucky, where Abe and Sarah had been born, the Lincolns moved there when Abe was two years old and stayed until he was almost eight. Their cabin was small and simple, constructed from lumber, mud, and stones found in the immediate area. Through the lower acres ran a clear, swift stream where Abe learned to fish and where his friend Austin Gollaher once saved him from drowning.

Did Abe ever see slaves when he lived at Knob Creek?

The Louisville-Nashville Pike (also known as the Cumberland Trail) was not far from the Lincoln's cabin. On this well-worn dirt road, Abe certainly saw all sorts of people passing by: traveling ministers, westward-bound families in covered wagons, and soldiers heading off to battle. Slavery was legal in Kentucky when Abe lived at Knob Creek, but his parents were against it. Although Abe made his first written account of slavery while traveling down the Mississippi at age nineteen, he probably had seen slaves being transported along the road that ran close to his Knob Creek home.

What was Abe's school like?

Education was a luxury on the frontier, and families considered themselves lucky to live close to a school. Usually, the schoolhouse itself was nothing more than a rough cabin with a single teacher who instructed the children in "readin', writin', and cipherin'" (arithmetic). The students—who were of all ages and often had to walk many miles to get there—sat side by side on hard, log benches, repeating their spelling, geography, and arithmetic lessons out loud. For this reason, they were called "blab schools." (Years later, when Abe ran a store and a post office, his business partner was annoyed by Abe's habit of reading the newspaper out loud.) Frontier schools had few books and almost no writing supplies except, perhaps, for a few pieces of chalk and several small slates. Just as often, children used a piece of coal and a wooden plank to practice their spelling and arithmetic.

During the cooler months, when Thomas could spare his son's help in the fields, Abe attended school as often as he could. Even so, Abe's formal education totaled less than a year. The fact that he became a respected lawyer, congressman, and one of our most eloquent presidents is largely the result of his own efforts.

If children only went to school sometimes, what did they do the rest of the time?

For a family to survive on the frontier, everyone had to help. As soon as their children could walk, parents taught them how to plant, weed, and tend to the garden; take care of livestock; haul water and wood; and gather berries and nuts. Older girls helped out with food preparation and the making and mending of clothes; older boys learned how to plow, chop wood, mend fences, and build furniture. They also learned how to fish and to hunt. Abe, perhaps because of his early losses, developed a sensitive spirit that made him opposed to any kind of cruelty. Although fishing in Knob Creek did not seem to trouble him, he did not like hunting. Only once did Abe shoot a wild animal for food—it was a wild turkey, and he felt so bad about it that he swore he would never shoot another living thing again.

What did kids in Abe's time do for fun?

Even hard-working frontier kids loved to play. Games that could be played with few or many children, and those that required little or no equipment, were the most popular. These included foot races and wrestling, stone throwing (for accuracy and distance), jump roping (using grapevines) and hoop rolling (using hickory saplings). Storytelling, singing, and making riddles were also popular after a long, tiring day of chores. As a teenager, Abe became known for his funny stories and his ability to mimic. When he stood on a tree stump imitating politicians, peddlers, and preachers he'd heard in town, he "brought belly-laughs" from his neighbors, who applauded his good humor.

In the story, who was the soldier Abe met on the road? Why was he fighting?

The "war with Great Britain" referred to in the 1890 Lincoln biography is more commonly known as "the war of 1812" or "the second war for independence." The war, which lasted until 1815, was fought for many reasons and on many fronts, mostly by American volunteers. In addition, because of the trade and expansion issues over which the war was waged, citizens from the southern and western states (such as Kentucky) supported the war much more than those living in the east.

The soldier Abe met on the road near Knob Creek was probably a Kentucky volunteer returning home from battles far to the north, near the Great Lakes and Canada. At that time, the American Army was made up mostly of local militia—a term that refers to ordinary citizens who supplied their own equipment and weapons. Many were farmers and tradesmen serving for short periods of time. When the fighting ended or the enemy moved on, they returned home to their farms, stores, or workshops. In the story, Abe's mother tells him to "be good to the soldiers," not only because they risk their lives, but also because they are people from families just like Abe's.

Roughly seventeen years later, in 1832, Abe joined the Illinois militia when they were needed to defend that state in the Black Hawk War. According to military records, he signed up three times for a period of thirty days each. When his enlistment was over, he began the long walk back. (His horse had been stolen, and he was several hundred miles from home.) I like to

imagine that, on the way, Abe may have met a generous boy willing to share his freshly caught fish!

When did Abe become president? What did he accomplish?

Abraham Lincoln was elected our sixteenth president, as well as our first Republican president, in November 1860. He led the United States through perhaps the most difficult years in its history. The United States was deeply divided over issues that included slavery and states' rights, which led to a civil war.

On January 1, 1863, President Lincoln signed the Emancipation Proclamation, which declared slaves (more than three million men, women, and children) in the Confederate states to be free. "I never, in my life, felt more certain that I was doing right, than I do in signing this paper," he said afterward.

In his Gettysburg Address in November 1863, Abe urged the country to come together in a "new birth of freedom" that would include equality for everyone and would guarantee that "government of the people, by the people, for the people, shall not perish from the earth."

In March 1865, Abe was elected to his second term as president. In his second inaugural speech, we can hear the poetic influence of his early books, especially the family Bible: "Fondly do we hope—fervently do we pray—that this mighty scourge of war may speedily pass away." One month later, on April 9, the civil war ended. Five days after that, Abe was shot by an assassin while watching a production at Ford's Theatre in Washington, D.C. He died the next morning.

Today, when the nation celebrates Lincoln's birth date, February 12, we remember the boy Abe from Knob Creek, who became a great leader and a true champion of freedom.

Selected Bibliography

Curtis, William Eleroy. *The True Abraham Lincoln.* Philadelphia: J. B. Lippincott Co., 1902, 1913.

Donald, David Herbert. *Lincoln.* New York: Simon & Schuster, 1995.

Fehrenbacher, Don and Virginia, eds. *Recollected Words of Abraham Lincoln.* Palo Alto, CA: Stanford University Press, 1996.

Harness, Cheryl. *Young Abe Lincoln: The Frontier Days 1809–1837.* Washington, DC: National Geographic Society, 1996.

Morgan, James. *Abraham Lincoln: The Boy and the Man.* New York: Grosset & Dunlap, 1908.

Nicolay, John G., and John Hay. *Abraham Lincoln: A History.* Vol. 1. New York: The Century Company, 1890.

Richardson, Robert Dale. *Abraham Lincoln's Autobiography with an Account of its Origins and History and Additional Biographical Material.* Boston: The Beacon Press, 1947.

Thomas, Benjamin P. *Abraham Lincoln: A Biography.* New York: Alfred A. Knopf, 1952.

Whipple, Wayne. *The Story-Life of Lincoln.* Philadelphia: The John C. Winston Co., 1908.

http://www.nps.gov/abli/index.htm (*National Park Service website of Abraham Lincoln's birthplace and boyhood home in Kentucky*)

http://ublib.buffalo.edu/libraries/eresources/ebooks/records/eep7832.html (*National Park Service website of the Lincoln Boyhood National Memorial in Indiana*)

To Find Out Even *More* About Abraham Lincoln:

Freedman, Russell. *Lincoln: A Photobiography.* New York: Clarion Books, 1987.

Meltzer, Milton, ed. *Lincoln, in His Own Words.* New York: Harcourt Brace & Co., 1993.

Phillips, E. B. *Abraham Lincoln: From Pioneer to President.* New York: Sterling Publishing Co., 2007.

St. George, Judith. *Stand Tall, Abe Lincoln.* Matt Faulkner, illustrator. New York: Philomel Books, 2008.

VanSteenwyk, Elizabeth. *When Abraham Talked to the Trees.* Bill Farnsworth, illustrator. Grand Rapids: Wm. B. Eerdmans, 2000.

Winters, Kay. *Abe Lincoln: The Boy Who Loved Books.* Nancy Carpenter, illustrator. New York: Simon & Schuster Books for Young Readers, 2003.

http://lincoln.lib.niu.edu (*The Abraham Lincoln Historical Digitation Project provides historical materials from Lincoln's Illinois years, 1830-1861, including his personal writings and public speeches.*)

http://www.apples4theteacher.com/holidays/presidents-day/abraham-lincoln/index.html (*This website includes games, activities, books and more about Abe Lincoln.*)

http://www.nps.gov/abli/planyourvisit/boyhood-home.htm (*Photos and information about Abe Lincoln's boyhood home at Knob Creek.*)

http://www.wku.edu/Library/museum/education/frontieronline (*Learn more about life on the Kentucky frontier by clicking on topics such as food, clothing, health, and folkways. This website also offers lesson plans and activities for the classroom.*)

Author's Acknowledgments

I am deeply grateful for the encouragement and assistance I received from the following people: Alyssa Eisner Henkin, literary agent, who brought the original anecdote to my attention and found the manuscript a wonderful home; Meredith Mundy Wasinger, editor, whose expert advice guided my shaping of this story for young readers; Scott Amerman, eagle-eyed production editor; Rod Blanton at the Abraham Lincoln Birthplace National Historical Monument, whose guidance regarding historical accuracy was invaluable; Kelley Clausing, a tireless researcher for The Papers of Abraham Lincoln in Springfield, Illinois (a project of the Illinois Historic Preservation Agency), who helped me track down an elusive bibliographic resource; and Karen Drickamer, special collections librarian at the Musselman Library at Gettysburg College, who provided me with helpful research, including pages from the first biography of Abraham Lincoln by Nicolay & Hay.

To Alyssa Eisner Henkin, with many thanks.
—J.B.

For my grandparents Theodore and Faye Barrett.
—A.J.B.

STERLING and the distinctive Sterling logo are
registered trademarks of Sterling Publishing Co., Inc.

Library of Congress Cataloging-in-Publication Data

Bryant, Jennifer.
Abe's fish : a boyhood tale of Abraham Lincoln / by Jen Bryant
illustrated by Amy June Bates.
p. cm.
Summary: Young Abe Lincoln learns the meaning of selflessness and freedom
when he encounters a soldier on a country road and gives up his prized possession:
a fish he caught for the family's evening meal. Includes author's note on the early
life of the sixteenth president.
Includes bibliographical references (p.).
ISBN 978-1-4027-6252-9
1. Lincoln, Abraham, 1809-1865—Childhood and youth—Juvenile fiction.
[1. Lincoln, Abraham, 1809-1865—Childhood and youth—Fiction.
2. Conduct of life—Fiction. 3. Freedom—Fiction.] I. Bates, Amy June, ill. II. Title.
PZ7.B8393Ab 2009
[E]—dc22
2008028597

2 4 6 8 10 9 7 5 3 1

Published by Sterling Publishing Co., Inc.
387 Park Avenue South, New York, NY 10016
Text copyright © 2009 by Jen Bryant
Illustrations copyright © 2009 by Amy June Bates

Distributed in Canada by Sterling Publishing
c/o Canadian Manda Group, 165 Dufferin Street
Toronto, Ontario, Canada M6K 3H6

Printed in China
All rights reserved

Sterling ISBN 978-1-4027-6252-9

The illustrations in this book were
rendered in pencil and watercolor
Designed by Scott Piehl

For information about custom editions, special sales,
premium and corporate purchases, please contact
Sterling Special Sales Department at 800-805-5489 or
specialsales@sterlingpublishing.com.

8/09

8/09